IT'S ALL ABOUT ME-OW

A Young Cat's Guide to the Good Life

HUDSON TALBOTT

Nancy Paulsen Books ◉ An Imprint of Penguin Group (USA) Inc.

To my muses—Claire, Sebastian, Dixie,
Poody, Picasso, Holly, and Jasper—
with gratitude for their inspiration

NANCY PAULSEN BOOKS · A division of Penguin Young Readers Group.
Published by The Penguin Group. Penguin Group (USA) Inc.,
375 Hudson Street, New York, NY 10014, U.S.A.
Penguin Group (Canada), 90 Eglinton Avenue East, Suite 700,
Toronto, Ontario M4P 2Y3, Canada (a division of Pearson Penguin Canada Inc.).
Penguin Books Ltd, 80 Strand, London WC2R 0RL, England.
Penguin Ireland, 25 St. Stephen's Green, Dublin 2, Ireland (a division of Penguin Books Ltd.).
Penguin Group (Australia), 250 Camberwell Road, Camberwell,
Victoria 3124, Australia (a division of Pearson Australia Group Pty Ltd).
Penguin Books India Pvt Ltd, 11 Community Centre, Panchsheel Park,
New Delhi - 110 017, India.
Penguin Group (NZ), 67 Apollo Drive, Rosedale, Auckland 0632, New Zealand
(a division of Pearson New Zealand Ltd).
Penguin Books (South Africa) (Pty) Ltd, 24 Sturdee Avenue,
Rosebank, Johannesburg 2196, South Africa.
Penguin Books Ltd, Registered Offices: 80 Strand, London WC2R 0RL, England.

Conceptual design by Hudson Talbott. Text set in Zemke Hand ITC.
The art was done in watercolors, colored pencil, and ink on Arches watercolor paper.
Library of Congress Cataloging-in-Publication Data
Talbott, Hudson.
It's all about me-ow : a young cat's guide to the good life / Hudson Talbott.   p. cm.
Summary: A cat gives three kittens advice on how to charm, entertain,
and communicate with their new human family. [1. Cats—Fiction. 2. Humorous stories.]
I. Title. II. Title: It's all about meow. III. Title: It is all about me-ow. PZ7.T153It 2012
[E]—dc23 2011050240
ISBN 978-0-399-25403-1
10 9 8 7 6 5 4 3 2 1

Welcome to your new home, fellow felines!
So now you've been weaned. Congratulations!

You're probably wondering:
How did I get here? Where's the food?

Who are those tall creatures
staring at me?

Those tall creatures are called "humans."

Except for that one. He's called "Here, boy."

They think that they are your new mommies.
(They've got the food.)

So that brings us to you!

You're probably feeling
a little helpless.
Yes, humans are big and
loud and kind of scary.
But look at them!
They're staring at you and
making goo-goo noises!

They want to make YOU happy!

Now's the time to take control!
You're probably saying,
"Me? How? Me? How?"

This is them . . .

Get the picture?
THEY NEED
OUR HELP!

But enough
about them.
Let's talk about us!

Ah, the wonders of being a CAT!

We're lean, mean hunting machines—the coolest of the cool!
Check out our fabulous feline features!

EYES

Day

Night

Built-in sunglasses control light

EARS

Pivot to pick up sounds, like radar

Hey, Fatso!

PAWS 'N' CLAWS

In   Out

WHISKERS
Help us feel our way through life.

PURRING
Saying so much with so little.

BACK
Has 29 more bones than human spine. More bones, more flexibility.

SOFT PADS
Keep us walking silently.

TAIL
Good for balance,
great for attitude.

Okay,
I'm walking
along
a rooftop.

Oops,
I'm falling!

Just
Kidding!
...sort of.

Looking
for
ground...

...landing
gear
down...

Relax,
prepare
for...

another
perfect
four-point
landing.

Cats rule!
Dogs drool!

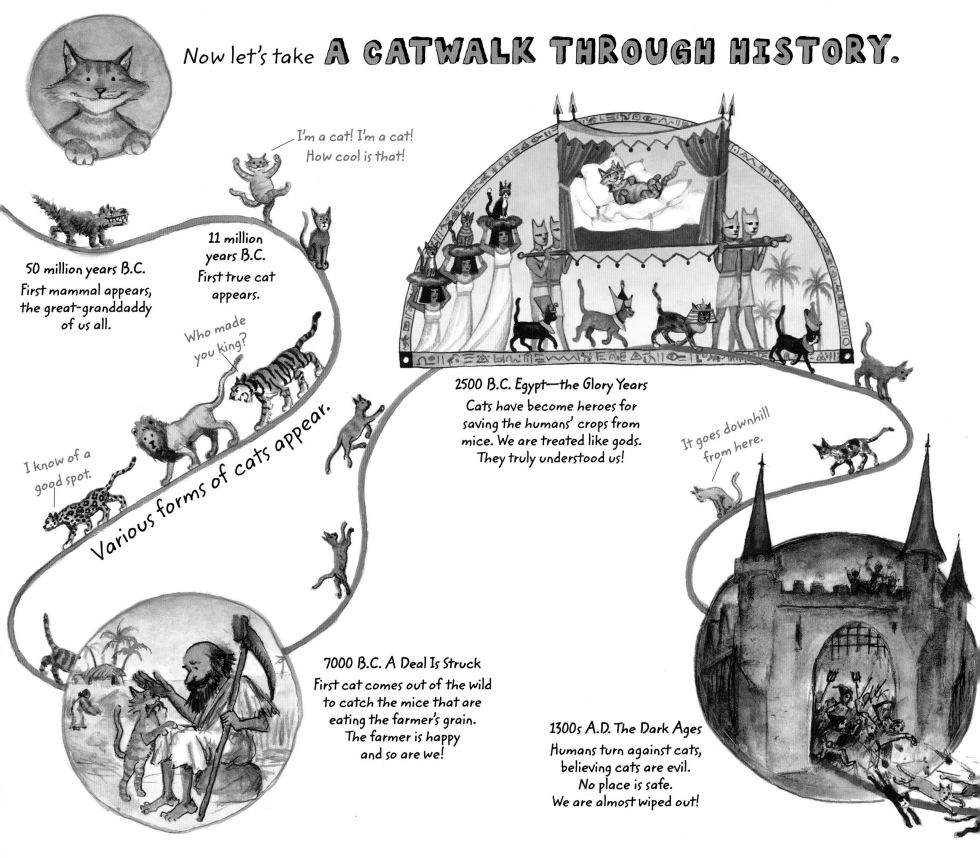

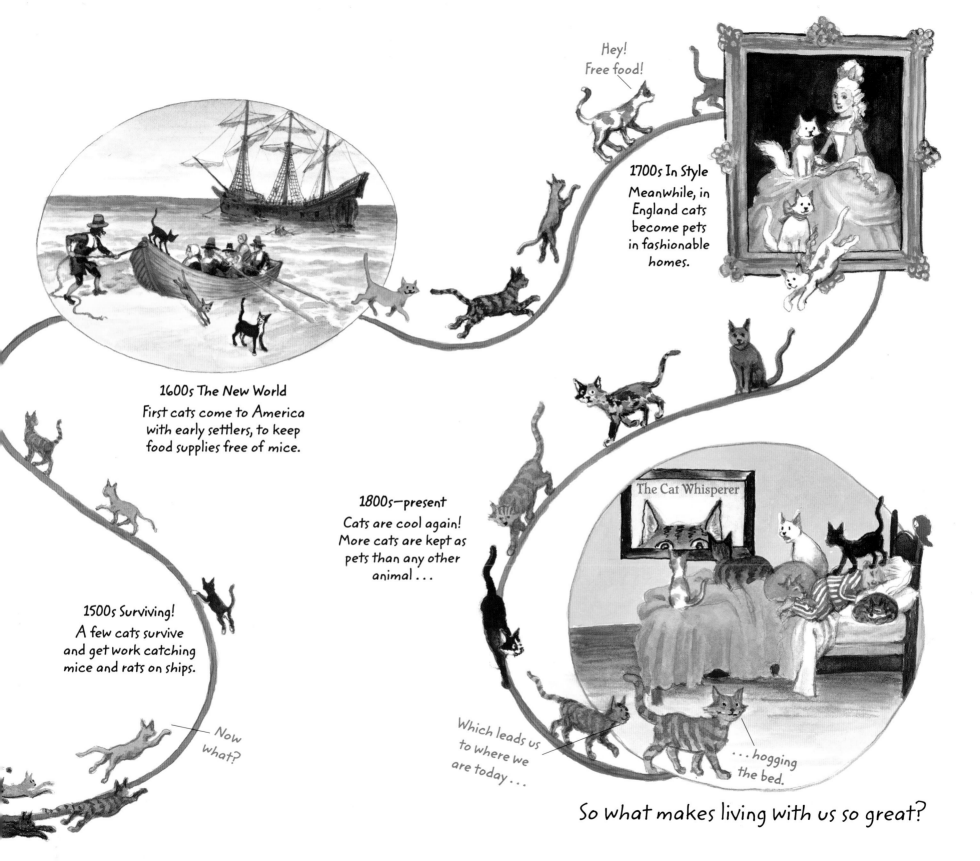

Hey!
Free food!

1700s In Style
Meanwhile, in England cats become pets in fashionable homes.

1600s The New World
First cats come to America with early settlers, to keep food supplies free of mice.

1800s—present
Cats are cool again! More cats are kept as pets than any other animal . . .

1500s Surviving!
A few cats survive and get work catching mice and rats on ships.

Now what?

The Cat Whisperer

Which leads us to where we are today . . .

. . . hogging the bed.

So what makes living with us so great?

Studies have shown the value of **PURR THERAPY** on the modern family.

Here's a family in need of purr therapy.

Here's a family getting purr therapy . . . any questions?

Not a bad life, eh?
We don't do tricks, we don't come when we're called,
we eat and sleep when we want to . . .
and yet, they love us for it! Why?

It's a little something I call . . .

...CATITUDE.

It's our way of being our way.
We make them smile and laugh
and feel all warm and fuzzy
because we ARE warm and fuzzy.

It's knowing when
to turn on the charm . . .

. . . or how to take a nap
with style . . .

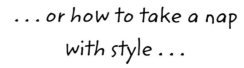

Catitude is the way
we make the world
our playground . . .

. . . and turn a household
from drab to fab!

Putting our personal
touch on everything . . .

from the dinner dishes

to the living room rug.

It's a big job. But somehow . . .

That Buddy! Warming my chair and so tired he fell asleep! I'll just sit somewhere else.

Goo-goo Mama.

Goo-goo Buddy.

I wonder if Buddy wants salmon or veal for dinner.

THE SYSTEM

WORKS!

Wait till Buddy sees the fish I caught for him!

Buddy, my role model!

I think Buddy needs more toys.

To keep the system working, we must first master the language.
I call it communi-**CAT**-ing.
Let's start with these simple phrases:

Whether you run into a mean cat, a nasty dog, or you just want to look good for Halloween, it's important to know how to empower yourself, with style.

fur up

tail up

BACK OFF!

Put your back into it!

Tail higher!

Are you a scaredy-cat or a SCARY CAT?

Once you've learned the basics of communi-CAT-ing, you're free to do your most important job . . .

IN AND OUT

Ask to go out | then to come in | ...then out... | ...in... | ...out... | ...in... | ...etc.... | etc.!

PET THE TUMMY — TRAP THE HAND

This pose says: "My tummy needs patting!...

And my teeth and claws need practice!"

Come on, I dare ya!

HUMANS MAY FORGET THAT YOU ARE THE CENTER OF THEIR WORLD.

Here's how to fix the problem:

Stare at them—
They'll wonder
why, but
you won't
tell them.

Sit in
unexpected places.

Stop eating your favorite food,
even if you're hungry.
You have to keep
them guessing.

Race wildly around the
house for no reason.

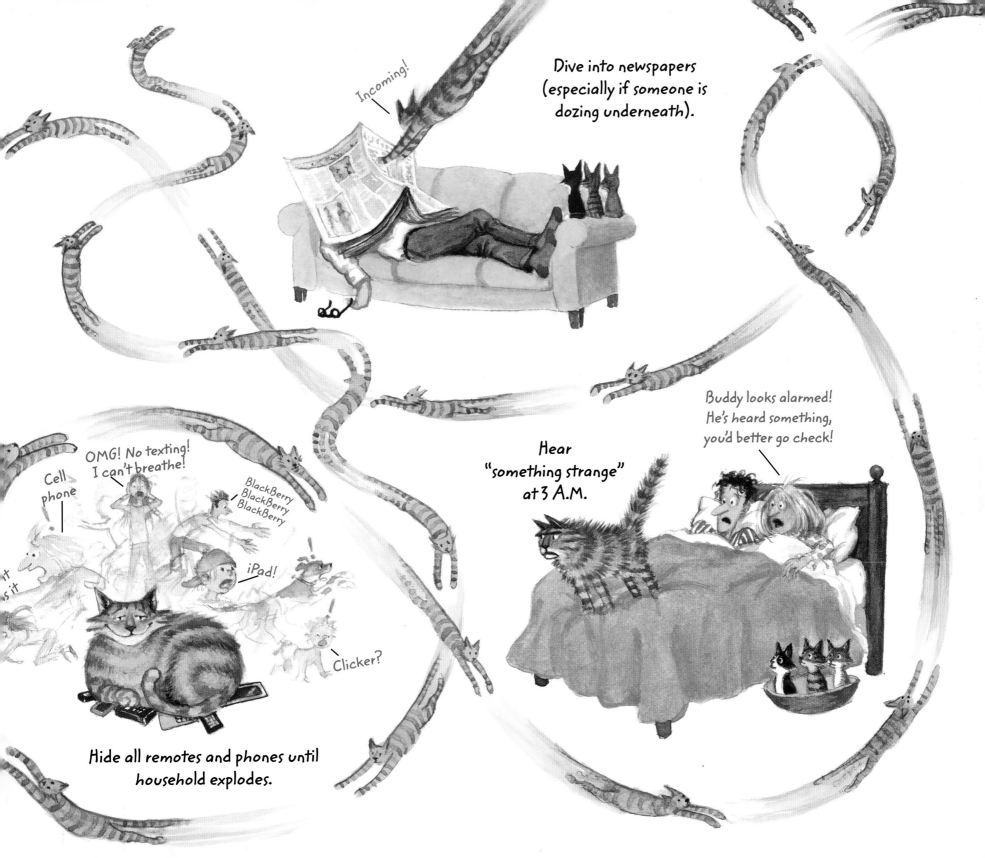

Incoming!

Dive into newspapers
(especially if someone is
dozing underneath).

OMG! No texting!
I can't breathe!

Cell
phone

BlackBerry
BlackBerry
BlackBerry

iPad!

Clicker?

Hide all remotes and phones until
household explodes.

Hear
"something strange"
at 3 A.M.

Buddy looks alarmed!
He's heard something,
you'd better go check!

Some humans need special training to be reminded when it's dinnertime.

For faster service, let your EYES do the talking.

What's for dinner?

Beginner

I need food.

Intermediate

Please!
Must . . . have . . .
fooooooo . . . o . . . d . . .

Advanced

Put the chicken in the bowl,
put the chicken in the bowl,
put the chicken in the bowl. . . .

Expert

Dining out? It's fun, but don't try sharing it with your humans.
Before bringing home your next trophy, learn these
DOs and **DON'T**s.

DO = Catch **DON'T** = Don't catch

mouse
DO

gerbil
DON'T

rat
DO

bunny
DON'T

(unless he's eating
the garden, then DO)

fish in a creek
DO

fish in a bowl
DON'T

snake
DO

(but don't bring him in the house)

Finally, my fellow felines,
some words of wisdom:

KEEP YOUR OUTSIDE MILD, BUT YOUR INSIDE WILD.

And sometimes we need
to let our inner kitty out.

That's what makes us cats—fur, freedom and . . .

OUR FABULOUS FAMILY!

Yep, those are all our crazy cousins.
What a beautiful bunch of beasties!

Family photo

Top Row (left to right)
cheetah
cougar with cubs
jaguar with cub
lynx (below jaguar)
leopard (black)
lion (Uncle Leo)
snow leopard (below lion)
caracal
tiger
leopard

Bottom Row (left to right)
Kentucky Wildcat
Angora with kittens
Abyssinian
Russian blue
Ragdoll
bicolored shorthair
American tabby
Persian
Maine coon
Siamese
ocelot

Okay, hold it, everybody!

GO CATS

CAT

... and when it's time for breakfast.

Isn't a cat's life purrrrrrrrrrrrrrrrfect?